DRUGS AND STRESS

Everyday routines and schedules create a certain amount of stress.

DRUGS AND STRESS

M.W. Buckalew, Jr.

THE ROSEN PUBLISHING GROUP, INC.
NEW YORK

For Erin and Adam

The people pictured in this book are only models; they, in no way, practice or endorse the activities illustrated. Captions serve only to explain the subjects of the photographs and do not imply a connection between the real-life models and the staged situations shown. News agency photographs are exceptions.

Published in 1993 by The Rosen Publishing Group, Inc.
29 East 21st Street, New York, NY 10010

First Edition

Manufactured in the United States of America

Library of Congress Cataloging-in-Publication Data

Buckalew, M.W.
    Drugs and stress / M.W. Buckalew, Jr.
       p.   cm. — (The Drug abuse prevention library)
    Includes bibliographical references and index.
    Summary: Discusses the dangers of specific drugs, explains how taking drugs to relieve tension or stress is likely to reinforce the problems and create greater stress, and suggests healthy ways to handle stress.
       ISBN 0-8239-1418-6
       1. Drug abuse. 2. Teenagers—Drug use.
       3. Stress in adolescence.
       [1. Drug abuse.] I. Title. II. Series
       HV5809.5.B83 1993
       362.29'0835—dc20   93-20288
                                         CIP
                                         AC

Contents

Introduction

My kids took me to a movie last night. The movie was "Pump Up the Volume," and it was about a high school student who starts a late-night radio show in his basement at home. Since he is good at talking to kids his age, they all turn on their radios and listen to him each night. Near the end, when he has been chased by the police and caught, he says to everyone, "I know high school is the pits. Being a teenager sucks."

A lot of adults forget that. Many adults, when thinking back about high school, seem to remember having a good time. They remember having a lot of friends. They remember falling in love. They remember nice teachers or coaches.

They forget the bad times. They forget how many kids did not like them. They forget how some kids ignored them. They forget how many girls or boys did *not* fall in love with them. They forget how many teachers made life hard. They forget how many coaches took away the fun of sports.

A good word to use to express your feelings when you think about the bad times at school and at home is *stress*. It can mean being worried. It can mean being angry. It can mean being scared. It can mean being unhappy.

Adults talk a lot about stress—for adults. They do not talk so much about stress for students. This book will talk about your stress and about how drugs often become part of your life even if you did not want them to.

Did you know that most Americans are "on drugs" right now? It's true. Most Americans are having, or have just had, a cup of coffee, a soda, a cigarette, a pill, or a drink (of alcohol). All these contain drugs. They make people "feel different." That's why people take them.

In this book I will talk about making your life good. I will talk about making your life good while you are still in high school and when high school is over. Making life good means, partly, knowing what stress is and knowing what to do about it.

Stress may be the result of built-up pressures and worries.

What Is Stress?

Lou Holtz is the football coach at the University of Notre Dame. Here is a story he likes to tell:

"A very rich man in Texas decided to have a party at his ranch. He didn't want anybody to swim in his pool, so he filled it with sharks.

"When everyone got there, he made a short speech. He said, 'I like to see people being brave. There is not enough bravery in our country today. If any of you are brave enough, dive into that pool and swim through all of those sharks. If you succeed, I will give you your choice of three wishes: my daughter's hand in marriage, the keys to my ranch, or a million dollars in cash. Is anyone brave enough to try it?'

"No one moved.

"Finally he turned to walk into his house. No sooner had he turned his back than he heard a splash! For twenty-two minutes a young man fought his way through the sharks before he reached the other side of the pool and climbed out. The ranch owner walked over to the tired young man and said, 'You are the bravest young man I have ever known. I am a man of my word, so I will give you your wish. You may have my daughter's hand in marriage, the keys to my ranch, or a million dollars in cash. Tell me—what is your wish?'

"The young man was silent for a few moments. Then he spoke. He said, 'Sir, my wish...is to know...who pushed me into that pool.'"

Recognizing Stress

Coach Holtz's story shows the problem. You cannot avoid stress, because it comes from inside yourself. Think about facing the tough guys in the hall. Think about being called on in class. Think about trying to write a paper for English class.

Think about not having enough money to buy something you really want.

All those things are called *stressors*. And the way you react to them is stress. When you worry about something, your body changes in an effort to cope with the problem.

Your body makes hormones, chemicals that flow through your blood and change the way you feel. They make you feel tense and uptight. They make butterflies in your stomach. Your heart may pound, your voice may become shaky, and your hands may feel cold. And all that makes it hard to think clearly.

The hormones are getting you ready to fight for your life or to run for your life. That is what stress really is. Your mind thinks about something that worries or upsets you, and your body feels stress. Faster than you can even talk about it, your body is ready to fight or to run, but your mind is no longer able to do anything very well.

And so you set yourself up to fail. The truth is that when you cannot think very clearly, you cannot do well. You fail tests. You say the wrong thing to a boy or girl you like. If you can't think well, you fail.

12 | *Another Problem*

Besides making it hard to think well, those same hormones in your blood can also make you quite sick. Often, they can keep your sickness defense from working. The germs that can make you sick are usually killed by your sickness defense, called your immune system.

But stress keeps your immune system from fighting the germs. So you get sick.

Think about it. Remember the last time you had a cold or the flu? Was something stressful going on in your life at that time? It's quite likely that you got the cold just before or during or after something that stressed you. You worry about something, the hormones stay in your blood for a while, and you get sick.

The Good Part

But stress can sometimes also help you. If you are facing a deadline to turn in a paper, the hormones can help you adapt to the extra demand on you. Many people say they work best when on a deadline. Many athletes turn in their best perform-ances when facing stiff competition. The so-called fight-or-flight reaction gives the quarterback the extra burst of energy to score the winning touchdown.

Athletes like Carl Lewis work with stress to help them win in competition.

14   So the trick in managing your stress is understanding what is going on in your body. If you feel under stress, ask yourself a few questions: What is the worst thing that can happen? (Probably nothing very bad!) Have I done everything I can to make the situation come out right? Will I remember it a few years from now?

People who do not understand stress and who let themselves give in to it may be tempted to try dangerous ways to get rid of it. They may make everything worse by turning to drugs.

CHAPTER 2

Taking Drugs: A Good Idea or Not?

*L*en Bias was the greatest basketball player in the history of the University of Maryland. He was smart. He was a true leader. He was a good student. He was an All-American.

When Len finished his college career, he was drafted by the Boston Celtics, a professional basketball team. The Celtics flew Len Bias to Boston. He was on TV and in all the newspapers. His family and friends were so proud of him.

Len signed a contract to play for the Celtics. The money from the contract would make him a millionaire. And he was barely twenty years old!

16 Len flew back to the University of Maryland. That night he was with several of his best friends. They were happy for him, and they all talked about the future and how it would be.

They decided to use some drugs. Why? Weren't they happy enough without taking something to make them "feel different"? No one knows. We only know that Len used cocaine. And we know that in just a few seconds the cocaine killed Len Bias.

So Len never got to see his wonderful future. He just died there in his college dorm room. His name was known by almost every person in America who read the sports pages. Now Len is just a memory.

Getting Messed Up

Not every person who uses drugs dies. Some do die. Others just get messed up. Sports stars, movie stars, singing stars, other famous people—and thousands of people whose names you never heard—get messed up from drugs every year. What does "messed up" mean? It means that their lives stop working, and if they are lucky, they go someplace where people can help them to "be human" again. It means that they begin to "need" their drugs, and

Drugs may lead to loss of control over your life.

18

that without the drugs they are not able to feel "right." It can mean that they become addicted to a drug, meaning that they need more and more of it or else they feel awful all the time.

An addict is a person who must have more and more of a drug and feels worse and worse without it. The addiction becomes the only thing in life that matters. People can be addicted to drugs, or they can be addicted to alcohol. There really is not much difference. If you become an addict, your life will be messed up—maybe forever.

Slick

Grace Slick was a famous singer in the 1960s and 1970s. She was the lead female voice with Jefferson Airplane, a popular band of the time. In 1990 she wrote an article in *Newsweek* magazine about herself and her teenage daughter.

Grace says that as a kid she used to watch her father drink. "He would sing, laugh, and generally enjoy himself when he got loaded," she says. "Looked like a good deal to me. Of course, I didn't have to feel the pain the next morning. I didn't feel the . . . loneliness that every alcoholic or addict experiences sooner or later."

So Grace learned to drink and to use drugs. She learned to feel bad all the time unless she had her drugs and alcohol. She learned to feel lonely.

Grace writes that her daughter was an alcoholic by the time she was only sixteen. Her daughter began to go to meetings of AA, a group that has helped hundreds of thousands of people over the years, and she has been sober for three years now, at age nineteen.

Grace Slick did not die as Len Bias did. She is fifty years old. She says, "Long-term peace—except maybe 'rest in peace'—is not found in a chemical."

Peer Pressure

No one will ever know exactly why Len Bias used cocaine. Some people said it was the first time he had ever tried it. Was it because his friends urged him to do it? Did they say, "Come on, Len, don't be a drag! Try it—you'll like it"?

That kind of urging by friends is called peer pressure. Such pressure can be very stressful even if it does not concern drugs.

Part of the teenage picture is the pressure to be like everyone else. And a very special part of being a teenager is wanting to be liked, to fit in, to be part of

Teens who don't smoke, drink, or do drugs have to resist peer pressure.

22 the gang. Peer pressure can lead you in good directions or bad. It can make you work extra hard to make the grades that your clique considers the "in" thing to do. Or it can make you listen to a friend who suggests "picking up" a lipstick at the cosmetics counter or an all-purpose scout knife in the sports department.

Good or bad, however, peer pressure is strong among teenagers. And it can be stressful. Controlled stress helps you get the A grade. And harmful stress can come from listening to your friend who thought stealing was okay.

Drugs?

Teenagers are starting to agree. The most recent report shows that high school seniors are less likely to use drugs now than in the last 15 years. The Office of National Drug Control Policy made a survey in 1990. It was called *Leading Drug Indicators*. It showed the following:

**Percent of High School Seniors
Using Drugs in Last 30 Days**
1975 — 30% of high school seniors
recently used drugs
1977 — 38% used drugs

1979 — 38% used drugs
1981 — 38% used drugs
1983 — 30% used drugs
1985 — 29% used drugs
1987 — 25% used drugs
1989 — 20% used drugs

In the Introduction we said that most Americans use drugs all of the time. Americans drink coffee and sodas, smoke cigarettes, take pills, and drink alcohol. All those things have drugs in them, so they all make you "feel different." And that, we said, is why people take them.

The numbers about high school seniors using drugs are not about coffee or sodas or cigarettes or pills or alcohol. Those numbers are about marijuana and Quaaludes and LSD and cocaine and heroin and other illegal drugs. The main difference between the first group of drugs (coffee, sodas, cigarettes, pills like Valium or Darvon, and alcohol) and the second group is mainly that the first group is legal and the second group is not legal.

Why? For many reasons. Some would say that the second group is much more dangerous. But that depends on what you really mean by "dangerous." Alcohol, for example, is a cause of 25,000 deaths in car

Coffee, alcohol, cigarettes, and other everyday drugs all have an
effect on the body's systems.

wrecks every year. Alcohol is also a cause
of 15,000 murders and suicides every year.

In fact, one ranking of drugs in order of their danger to humans goes like this:

1. Alcohol
2. Nicotine (cigarettes)
3. Drugs (legal ones like Valium or Darvon)
4. Drugs (illegal ones like cocaine or heroin)
5. Sodas, coffee (and other food or drink containing "additives")

It is hard to say which drugs are the most dangerous. Almost all can kill you in one way or another.

Len Bias died from a tiny bit of cocaine. People may drink a lot of alcohol before it kills them. But try this—try thinking more about life than about death.

What Is a Good Life?

Is your life good? Is it going to be good someday? Let's take a look at that.

Here is a list of the 10 Top Worries among teenagers. The list tells us what teenagers mean when they talk about a good life.

1. Having a good marriage and family life

2. Choosing the right job or finding steady work
3. Doing well in school
4. Doing well in a job or line of work
5. Having good friends
6. Paying for college
7. America "going downhill"
8. Making a lot of money
9. Finding goals and meaning in life
10. Getting AIDS

Those are the things teenagers worry about the most. What drugs will help you with your 10 Top Worries? The answer should be clear to you.

None of the illegal ones can help, can they? They can only keep you from having a good marriage or a good family life or choosing the right job or finding steady work or doing well in school or being successful or having friends or almost anything else that would be good in life.

Can any of the legal ones help at all? Probably not. But we do see (on TV, at least) people with good jobs, nice clothes, and money drinking alcohol, coffee, or soda. So is there a problem with those drugs—outside of alcohol being a cause of 40,000 deaths a year, or cigarettes being a main cause of lung cancer, heart attacks, and other deaths?

Yes. There is a problem.

What's the Problem?

Any drug—even the ones in sodas, coffee, and headache pills—can be a problem if you use it all the time. You begin to "need" it in your mind, and maybe in your body. You are no longer in control of yourself. *Being out of control is the most stressful way to be.*

You are stressed when you do not have control of what happens to you.

No one plans to be an addict. No one plans to become addicted to soda, coffee, pills, alcohol, cigarettes, marijuana, LSD, Quaaludes, cocaine, heroin, or anything else. It just happens. It happens a lot faster than you might think.

By the time you realize that you are hooked on a drug, it is too late to stop easily. Stopping will take time and effort and, maybe, help from other people. And it will be stressful.

It's weird, isn't it? People take drugs because they feel stressed. Taking drugs soon makes them more stressed than they were before. And then stopping the drugs is even more stressful for a while. It

28 would make a lot more sense to learn to handle stress *without* drugs.

Wouldn't it?

A True Story

A teacher showed a school principal a bottle of torn leaves. The teacher had thought the leaves were marijuana, an illegal drug. He had seen two students, both of them fourteen years old, playing with the bottle. He had taken it from them, giving it to the principal with the boys' names.

The principal then did what he had to do. The law said that he had to call the state police. So he did that.

The law said that he had to call the city police. So he did that, too.

Other rules said that he had to call the boys' parents. So he did that.

Can you picture that? In less than fifteen minutes after the teacher took the bottle of marijuana, the state police and the city police had the boys' names. The boys' parents had been told and were very upset. The law and the rules said all that had to happen right away. So it did.

The city police wanted to go to talk to the boys. They also thought that maybe

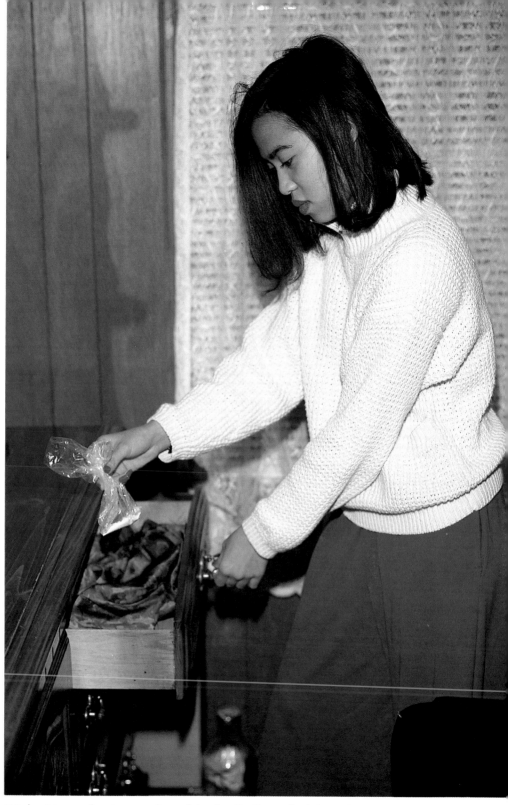

It is best to confront a member of the family if you find drugs in your home.

30 the boys should go to a reform school for "bad" boys and girls.

But the principal said no, not until he had talked to the boys. He had done what the law and the rules said he had to do. But now he wanted to talk to the boys himself.

He called them to his office. One of the boys said he did not know how the little bottle got to school. He had just looked at the bottle when the other boy showed it to him. His teacher said that was true.

The principal sent that boy out of the office and called the other boy in. That boy knew a lot about the little bottle. He had found it in the parking lot of a store where his family had stopped the night before. He had taken it home and had shown it to his mother. He had asked her what it was.

And what had his mother said was in the little bottle?

He said that his mother told him it was rabbit food.

"Rabbit food?"

"Yes, sir. Rabbit food."

His mother thought it was rabbit food. So he thought it was rabbit food, too. He liked the little bottle, so he took it to school to show his friend.

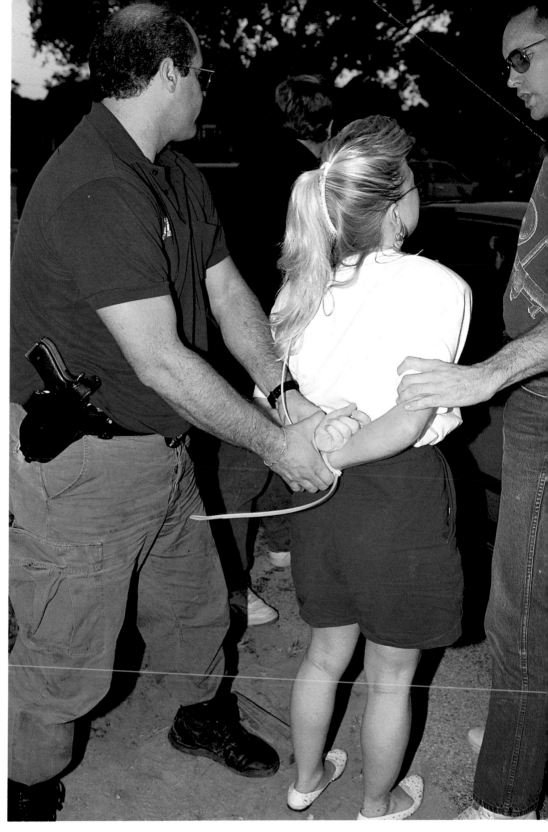

Possession of drugs may lead to arrest.

32 Rabbit food.

Finally the principal said to him, "That's not rabbit food. That is a drug called marijuana."

The principal watched the boy very closely. He wanted to know if the boy was telling the truth.

"Marijuana!" the boy cried. Tears popped into his eyes and ran down his cheeks. "Marijuana? No! Mom said it was rabbit food!"

The principal thought about what the boy had done. He was a smart young man. If he had known this was an illegal

Saying no to drugs is the best prevention against addiction.

drug, he would not have shown it to his mother. He would not have brought it to school and shown it to his friend while a teacher was standing next to him. He would not have been so quick to tell the principal where he found the bottle and what he had done with it.

The principal believed him. The boy really thought it was rabbit food.

The principal called the state police and the city police and told them what he thought. When the boys' parents got to the office, he told them as well.

So everything was fine.

Or was it?

Because of the law, the names of those two boys are now on file with the state police and the city police. Because of the law, both boys' parents had been very frightened and upset. That's the law. If you are seen with any illegal drug at all, something will happen to you. It does not matter that you thought it was rabbit food or something else. Something will happen anyway.

And remember this. If the principal had not believed the boy, the police would have come to see him. The boy would have gone to court. If a judge had not believed him, he might have been sent to

34 reform school. His whole life could have been changed just because he picked up a little bottle of torn leaves in a parking lot.

Illegal drugs can get you in very big trouble very, very quickly. Even if you don't know what you are seeing or doing, you can be in very big trouble. Think about it.

Just Say No?

What do you think? We have talked about stress. We have talked about how people use drugs because they are stressed. We have talked about how using drugs soon makes people much more stressed than they were before. We have talked about how trying to stop using drugs is the most stressful thing of all.

And we have read a true story about what it can be like to be "caught" with an illegal drug.

Drugs can kill you.

But it's worse than that. Drugs can make your life terrible long before they actually kill you.

Stress can mess you up. Stress can make you fail. Stress can make you sick. But you *can* handle stress without drugs. And that makes a lot more sense.

CHAPTER 3

Making Your Life Good

A famous teacher once studied dogs. Dogs act like people sometimes. We know right away when a dog is happy, or scared, or mad, or confused.

The teacher studied dogs who were kept in a small room (in his lab) with no doors or windows. At first the dogs tried to get out. When they learned that there was no way out, they gave up. They just sat there.

When the teacher put the dogs in a small room with a window, they still just sat there. They had learned that you can't get out of a small room, so they didn't try.

Finally the teacher put the dogs in a small room with an open door. An open door! And still the dogs just sat there. They had learned that you can't get out of a small room, so they didn't try.

36 The teacher noticed that people are the same way. When people find out that they can't do something, they stop trying. They often stop trying to do anything at all just because they can't do one thing.

How about you? Have you stopped trying to do everything just because you can't yet do one thing? It is easy to begin to feel that you can't make it.

In Chapter 2 we talked about the fact that being out of control is the most stressful way to be. That is why school is stressful. You are not in control of what happens to you there. In school you may find that reading is hard, and so you may feel that everything is hard—too hard.

That is what the teacher meant when he said that dogs *and* people stop trying when they find they can't do something. They stop trying to do anything at all.

Being in control means feeling that you can learn to do anything you really want to do. When you learn to have that feeling, nothing is too stressful. You are sure that you can handle anything that comes your way. Remember our list of the 10 Top Worries among teenagers. Included in the list were marriage and jobs and school and friends and college and money.

Drug-free teens enjoy life and have positive attitudes.

38   Do you feel in control when you think of things like that? Do you feel that you know how to get those things? Or have you stopped trying?

The Heathen Angels

Several years ago a young man worked with a group of teenagers in California. Most of them were fifteen years old. Most of them were in the 10th grade. They formed a club called The Heathen Angels. They met twice a week. In their meetings they planned projects to help the old people where they lived. They planned dances. They planned trips.

They had a hero. The brother of one of them was a boxer. Sometimes they would go and watch him fight. He was good, but not good enough to become a champion.

The teenagers in this club were smart. They could read and write. They could do math. They were all in school.

But none of them had plans. Not really. Sure, the club would plan projects or trips or dances. But none of the teenagers had plans for themselves.

They did not want to think about what they might do after high school. One or two of them said they might want to be a

Being involved in positive activities creates joy and satisfaction.

boxer, like the older brother. Most of them did not want to think about it at all.

They had no goals. Why not? They had no goals because they had given up. They didn't want to try any longer. They felt they had no control over what might happen in their future. They did not think they could make a plan and then make the plan happen.

40

What About You?

Do you have a plan? Do you feel that you are in control of your future? Or have you given up, like those dogs?

Remember Coach Holtz's story about the sharks, and the pool, and getting pushed in? The fact that you have gotten as far as you have in school—swimming through the sharks every day—says that you can reach goals if you set them and that you can be in control of your life.

Coach Holtz also tells a true story about himself. When he was about thirty years old, he lost his job. He already had a family with three children, but he had no job with which to support them.

He didn't know what to do. He could not control what was happening to him. He was stressed. He could have given up. He could have turned to drugs. He could have left his family.

He did not do those things.. Instead, he thought for several weeks about his life and about how to make his life good.

Then he set goals for his life. He set 107 goals! Some of his goals were funny, like jumping out of an airplane. But most of his goals were not very funny at all, like someday becoming Notre Dame's head football coach.

It takes steady, hard work to reach the goals you set in life.

Lou Holtz went from having no job at age thirty to being head football coach at Notre Dame in about twenty years. To do that, he had to believe in himself. Even when he had no job at all, he had to believe in himself.

There is no better way to make your life good than to set goals for yourself, and believe in yourself, and then to work to reach your goals. There are no shortcuts.

Hooks for Your Hopes

You need three hooks on which to hang your hopes for making your life good:

- You need goals for yourself.
- You need a high school diploma.
- You need an adult you can trust.

Goals? Think about the 10 Top Worries list. Turn back to Chapter 2 and look at it again. There is one thing that affects nearly every item on the list. This is your education.

If you are in high school right now, and if you are able to read this book, you can graduate from high school. You can also probably graduate from a two-year or a four-year college. And you can probably make your whole life as good as you want to make it.

A few years ago a group of teachers studied people who had made good lives. What do you think those people had in common?

The main thing was that they all got a college degree, which means that they also got a high school diploma. It did not matter how much money their families had or did not have. It did not matter how good their grades were in high school, as long as they were able to graduate. It did not matter what college they attended. It did not matter whether or not they had to borrow money to go to college.

It just mattered that they went, and they finished.

How can you do that? How can you graduate from high school, go to a two-year or a four-year college, and graduate from that school, too?

You can learn to read as well as you can. You can learn to handle the stress of it all, so that you can do well in tests and not get sick while you are working toward this goal. You can learn that you must stay in control of you. That means that you must know that drugs cannot help you and will almost surely keep you from your goal.

Remember, the first two "Hooks for Your Hopes" are setting solid goals and

44 graduating from school. We have just agreed that these two "hooks" are really parts of one thing: your education. If your education is your main goal, you have two of your three "Hooks for Your Hopes."

What about that third "hook"—an adult you can trust? Why is that important? It is important because any student, no matter how smart, needs to be able to talk to someone who has gone through high school and college and can help.

With a pencil and paper, make a list of numbers 1 through 17. Go through the list of "Adults You Can Trust." Make a check mark beside any adult who is a good listener or friendly or available to you.

Really think about this. It is important. You will do much better with your first two "Hooks for Your Hopes" if you also have this third "hook."

Did any adults on your list have three check marks? Were there any with two? Those adults are the ones to whom you should seriously consider talking.

If no adults on your list have two or three check marks, you need to choose one of your teachers or coaches or counselors or principals and explain that you need an adult you can trust.

Adults You Can Trust

Good Listener   Friendly   Available

1. Mother or stepmother or foster mother _____

2. Father or stepfather or foster father _____

3. Adult sister or brother _____

4. Aunt or uncle _____

5. Grandmother or grandfather _____

6. Adult relative other than the above _____

7. A teacher _____

8. A counselor _____

9. A principal _____

10. A coach _____

11. A music director (or other director of special activities) _____

12. A minister, priest, or rabbi _____

13. A neighbor _____

14. An adult "boss" at your summer or after-school job _____

15. An admissions counselor at any college of interest to you _____

16. Other professional "helpers" _____

17. Any other adults (list by name): _____

Finding someone to talk to can be the first step in recovering from a drug problem.

If that sounds too hard, *just ask him or her to read this book*. That will make it clear. In fact, that is the best way to make it clear to any adult.

What will the trusted adult do for you? First of all, he or she will listen to you. And you must talk. You must tell this person why you have decided that your education is important to you now.

Say that you want to stay in control of your life. Say that you want to make your life good, that you want to be able to handle the stress of life, and that you want no part of drugs.

Your trusted adult can probably take it from there. He or she can help you look at the courses you are taking in high school. He or she can help you learn how to take tests better. He or she can help you get help with your reading skills. He or she can help you think about college. He or she can help you get information on how to get in and how to get help with the money problems that all students have when they go to college.

Your trusted adult can be of great help to you in meeting your goals. Choose one. Take this book with you. Talk to him or her. *It will be worth the effort*.

Daily physical exercise can be helpful in relieving stress.

CHAPTER 4

Winning

We have talked about drugs. We have talked about stress and about being in control. We have talked about goals. We have talked about your education and about your trusted adult.

Now it is time to think harder about stress control. We have seen what stress can do: It makes you fail; it makes you sick. We have seen that using drugs just makes stress worse. We have seen that using drugs means that you will fail for sure, and in worse ways. We have seen that learning to handle stress puts you in control.

This chapter is called "Winning" because if you learn stress control, you

50 can win in anything. How? By winning over yourself. Stress will defeat you if you let it. Stress control allows you to defeat stress and to be at your best.

Do you play basketball? Do you watch other people play basketball? Think about the last time you shot a free throw or saw someone else shoot a free throw. What happened just before you made the shot after the referee gave you the ball?

Probably you or the player you watched took hold of the ball. You took one or two very deep breaths, relaxed the hand and arm you were going to shoot with, and *then* you shot.

Did the shot go in? Maybe. It doesn't really matter. But somehow you knew that it was more likely to go in if you first took deep breaths and relaxed your arm. So the first thing you did was to defeat your stress. Then you shot.

That was stress control.

Without it, you were likely to miss your shot. With it, you were more likely to make it.

The same is true in your classes and in anything else you do. With stress control, you are more likely to do well. Without stress control, you are less likely to do well.

All achievers deal with and manage stress on a daily basis. Here, the winners of the 42nd annual Westinghouse Science Talent Search, celebrate their achievements.

52   Remember in Chapter 1 we talked about upsetting thoughts that cause your body to make hormones. Those little drops in your blood make you feel tense and uptight. They make butterflies in your stomach. They make it very hard to *think* clearly.

How could a deep breath and a relaxed body do anything to help you? Normal breathing and a relaxed body keep your mind and body from getting more upset. Normal breathing and a relaxed body make your mind and body think that you are in control. You feel that you do not need more stress hormones in your blood. And so you have *controlled your stress*. You have done stress control. It is that simple.

How can you remember to do stress control when you are having worried or upsetting thoughts? One good way is called Counting Down.

To use Counting Down, think of your body as having three parts. Part Three is your face. Part Two is your body. Part One is your legs.

When you feel yourself starting to get worried, no matter where you are or what you are doing, say to yourself quickly, "Three, Two, One."

As you say "Three," relax your facial muscles (especially your jaw).

As you say "Two," take a very long, slow breath.

As you say "One," relax your legs.

That's it. That is one of the very best ways to do stress control. It takes only a couple of seconds. No one else knows you are doing it. You can do it a hundred times a day. It's easy. *And it works.*

It is *your* Counting Down and *your* stress control. And so it puts you back in control anytime *you* choose.

Drugs are of no use in making your life good. Stress control is. Being in control is. Having solid goals is. Getting your education is. Having a trusted adult is.

That is what winning really means. It means defeating stress and all the other things that can get in the way of making your life good. You can start winning. Just decide.

CHAPTER 5

Your Contract

*A*nytime you decide to change yourself, or to set goals, or to make your life better, you need to write it down. Everybody does.

We all do better that way. We see on paper what we have decided to do. We see on paper what steps we must take. And so we do better. We know what to do. And we know when we have done it.

A contract is just that. It is a promise to yourself, written on paper.

Following is a sample contract. Look at it carefully. Then make one for yourself. You don't need to show it to anyone except your trusted adult. You will want that person to see it so you can talk about it and think about it. That person can help **54** you make your contract happen.

A Sample Contract

For the three-month period starting ——————
and ending ——————— .

My Goals—

I. Education

    A. Homework: Each night before I go to sleep I will work on my *hardest* subject for 45 minutes (even if I could do it in less time).

    B. Homework: Each night before I go to sleep, I will read aloud from one of my school books for 30 minutes.

    C. Teachers: I will meet with every teacher I have to tell them that I want to do well and to give them a chance to tell me how I might improve. I will do this once every four weeks.

II. Drugs and Stress

    A. Every night I will pretend to be taking a test or talking to a teacher or something else stressful, and I will do Counting Down for practice.

    B. Every night I will think about how I can make sure that tomorrow will be drug-free for me—no contact with people who sell or use drugs, and no actions of any kind that will keep me from being in control of my own life.

Writing down your goals helps to keep you on track.

For your contract to work, you need to write it yourself. It can be as short as you want to make it, or as long. But you must remember, to succeed with goals, there should only be a few. Work on just a few things at a time. Get good at each goal. Then you can write a new one.

Look at your contract every single day to make sure you are doing what you have said you would. Talk to your trusted adult about it at least once a week. You must let that person help you. All of us do better if we can talk with someone we trust about our goals every day or every week.

This is all you need to start to make your life better and to be in control of what happens to you. Share this book with others who need to get control of their own lives. Talk with them about it. Get your friends to care about being in control of their lives. Help them. And help yourself.

You can do this.

Help List

AA (Alcoholics Anonymous)

Check your telephone book. Local AA offices in most areas are open 9 a.m.– 5 p.m. Many have a 24-hour hotline number.

CA (Cocaine Anonymous)
    1-213-559-5833

Drug and Alcohol Hotline
    1-800-252-6465

National Council on Alcoholism and Drug Dependency

    1-800-NCA-CALL, or
    1-800-622-2255

Institute on Black Chemical Abuse (IBCA)
    1-312-663-5780

Jewish Alcoholics, Chemically Dependent Persons and Significant Others (JACS)
    1-212-473-4747

National Asian Pacific Families Against Abuse
    1-301-530-0945

National Coalition of Hispanic Health and Human Services
    1-202-371-2100

Glossary

Explaining New Words

AA (Alcoholics Anonymous) Group of people who are addicted to alcohol and who meet often to help one another stay away from drinking.

addiction Need for more and more of a drug in order to feel "normal."

AIDS (acquired immune deficiency syndrome) Fatal disease caused by the human immunodeficiency virus (HIV). It is transmitted through blood and other body fluids, especially during sexual activity or intravenous drug use.

contract An agreement between people to do, or not to do, some action.

60 | **drug** Chemical substance that changes the functioning of the body. It may be used in the treatment of an illness or to alter the state of one's mind, as in illegal drugs.

goal An aim or a purpose toward which one works and which one hopes to achieve.

hormones Chemical substances that flow through your bloodstream and affect the activity of body organs.

immune system Body system that fights disease.

stress Pressure caused by the body's physical or emotional response to outside events.

For Further Reading

Ardel, Don, and Tager, Mark. *Planning for Wellness*. Dubuque, IA: Kendall/Hunt, 1982.

Ball, Jacqueline. *Everything You Need to Know about Drug Abuse*, rev. ed. New York: Rosen Publishing Group, 1992.

Edwards, Gabrielle. *Coping with Drug Abuse*, rev. ed. New York: Rosen Publishing Group, 1990.

Gooden, Kimberly Wood. *Coping with Family Stress*. New York: Rosen Publishing Group, 1989.

Keyishian, Elizabeth. *Everything You Need to Know about Smoking*, rev. ed. New York: Rosen Publishing Group, 1993.

62 Lazarus, Arnold, and Fay, Allen. *I Can If I Want To*. New York: Warner, 1977.

McFarland, Rhoda. *Coping with Substance Abuse*, rev. ed. New York: Rosen Publishing Group, 1990.

Sehnert, Keith. *Stress/Unstress*. Minneapolis, MN: Augsburg, 1981.

Stroebel, Charles. *OR: The Quieting Reflex*. New York: Berkley, 1982.

Tanner, Ogden, ed. *Stress*. New York: Time-Life Books, 1976.

Taylor, Barbara. *Everything You Need to Know about Alcohol*. New York: Rosen Publishing Group, 1988.

Index

About the Author
Dr. M. Walker Buckalew researches human stress and has taught courses in stress control for the Education Department of St. Lawrence University, Canton, New York. Prior to that, Dr. Buckalew spent six years teaching English and coaching a variety of sports. He is the author of several books on stress.

Photo Credits
Cover photo: Stuart Rabinowitz.
Pages 13, 51: Wide World Photos; page 31: © Roger M. Richards/Gamma-Liaison. All other photos by Stuart Rabinowitz.

Design & Production: Blackbirch Graphics, Inc.